'MISS X IS
WALKING
THE STREETS
OF THE CITY,
COMPLETELY
ALONE.'

SHIRLEY JACKSON
Born 1916, San Francisco, California, USA
Died 1965, North Bennington, Vermont, USA

'Journey with a Lady' was first published in *Harper's* in 1952, and 'The Missing Girl' in *Fantasy and Science Fiction* in 1957. Along with 'Nightmare', they appear in the collection *Just an Ordinary Day*, published posthumously in 1997.

JACKSON IN PENGUIN MODERN CLASSICS
*The Bird's Nest*
*Dark Tales*
*Hangsaman*
*The Haunting of Hill House*
*Just an Ordinary Day*
*Let Me Tell You*
*The Lottery and Other Stories*
*The Road Through the Wall*
*The Sundial*
*We Have Always Lived in the Castle*

**SHIRLEY JACKSON**

*The Missing Girl*

PENGUIN BOOKS

PENGUIN CLASSICS

UK | USA | Canada | Ireland | Australia
India | New Zealand | South Africa

Penguin Books is part of the Penguin Random House group
of companies whose addresses can be found at
global.penguinrandomhouse.com.

This selection first published 2018
001

Set in 10.25/12.75 pt Dante MT Std
Typeset by Jouve (UK), Milton Keynes
Printed in Great Britain by Clays Ltd, St Ives plc

ISBN: 978-0-241-33928-2

www.greenpenguin.co.uk

MIX
Paper from
responsible sources
FSC® C018179

Penguin Random House is committed to a
sustainable future for our business, our readers
and our planet. This book is made from Forest
Stewardship Council® certified paper.

# Contents

## The Missing Girl

She was humming, tunelessly, moving around somewhere in the room stirring things gently, and always humming. Betsy tightened her shoulders over the desk and bent her head emphatically over her book, hoping that her appearance of concentration would somehow communicate a desire for silence, but the humming went on. Debating a dramatic gesture, a wild throwing of the book to the floor, a shout of annoyance, Betsy thought as she had so often before, but you *can't* be cross with her, you just *can't*, and she bent farther over her book.

'Betsy?'

'Um?' Betsy, still trying to look as though she were studying, realized that she could have described every movement in the room until now.

'Listen, I'm going out.'

'Where? At this time of night?'

'I'm going out anyway. I've got something to do.'

'Go ahead,' Betsy said; just because one could not be cross, one need not necessarily be interested.

'See you later.'

The door slammed and Betsy, with relief and a feeling of freshness, went back to her book.

It was not, as a matter of fact, until the next night that anyone asked Betsy where her room-mate had gone. Even then it was casual, and hardly provoked Betsy to thought: 'You all alone tonight?' someone asked. 'She out?'

'Haven't seen her all day,' Betsy said.

The day after that, Betsy began to wonder a little, mostly because the other bed in the room had still not been slept in. The monstrous thought of going to the Camp Mother occurred to her ('Did you *hear* about Betsy? Went tearing off to old Auntie Jane to say her room-mate was missing, and here all the time the poor girl was . . .') and she spoke to several other people, wondering and curious, phrasing it each time as a sort of casual question; no one, it turned out, had seen her room-mate since the Monday night when she had told Betsy, 'See you later,' and left.

'You think I ought to go tell Old Jane?' Betsy asked someone on the third day.

'Well . . .' consideringly. 'You know, it might mean trouble for *you* if she's really missing.'

The Camp Mother, comfortable and tolerant and humorous, old enough to be the mother of any of the counselors, wise enough to give the strong impression of experience, listened carefully and asked, 'And you say she's been gone since Monday night? And here it is Thursday?'

'I didn't know what to do,' Betsy explained candidly; 'she could have gone home, or . . .'

'Or . . . ?' said the Camp Mother.

'She said she had something to do,' Betsy said.

Old Jane pulled her phone over and asked, 'What was her name again? Albert?'

'Alexander. Martha Alexander.'

'Get me the home of Martha Alexander,' Old Jane said into her phone, and from the room beyond, in the handsomely paneled building that served as the camp office and, at the other end, as kitchen, dining room, and general recreation room, Old Jane and Betsy could hear the voice of Miss Mills, Old Jane's assistant, saying irritably, 'Alexander, Alexander,' as she turned pages and opened filing drawers. 'Jane?' she called out suddenly, 'Martha Alexander from . . . ?'

'New York,' Betsy said. 'I *think.*'

'New York,' Old Jane said into her phone.

'Righto,' Miss Mills said from the other room.

'Missing since Monday,' Old Jane reminded herself, consulting the notes she had made on her desk pad. 'Said she had something to do. Picture?'

'I don't think so,' Betsy said uncertainly. 'I may have a snapshot somewhere.'

'Year?'

'Woodsprite, I *think*,' Betsy said. 'I'm a woodsprite, I mean, and they usually put woodsprites in with woodsprites and goblins in with goblins and senior huntsmen in with –' She stopped as the phone on Old Jane's desk rang and Old Jane picked it up and said briskly, 'Hello? Is this Mrs Alexander? This is Miss Nicholas calling from the Phillips Education Camp for Girls Twelve to Sixteen. Yes, that's right . . . Fine, Mrs

Alexander, and how are *you*? . . . Glad to hear it. Mrs Alexander, I'm calling to check on your daughter . . . Your *daughter*, Martha . . . Yes, that's right, Martha.' She raised her eyebrows at Betsy and continued. 'We're checking to make sure that she's come home or that you know where she is . . . yes, where she is. She left the camp very suddenly last Monday night and neglected to sign out at the main desk and of course our responsibility for our girls requires that even if she has only gone home we must –' She stopped, and her eyes focused, suddenly, on the far wall. 'She is not?' Old Jane asked. 'Do you know where she is, then? . . . How about friends? . . . Is there anyone who might know?'

The camp nurse, whose name was Hilda Scarlett and who was known as Will, had no record of Martha Alexander in the camp infirmary. She sat on the other side of Old Jane's desk, twisting her hands nervously and insisting that the only girls in the infirmary at that moment were a goblin with poison oak and a woodsprite with hysterics. 'I suppose you *know*,' she told Betsy, her voice rising, 'that if you had come to one of us the *minute* she *left* . . .'

'But I didn't *know*,' Betsy said helplessly. '*I* didn't know she was gone.'

'I am afraid,' said Old Jane ponderously, turning to regard Betsy with the air of one on whom an unnecessary and unkind burden has been thrust, 'I am very much afraid that we must notify the police.'

It was the first time the chief of police, a kindly family man whose name was Hook, had ever been required to visit a girls' camp; his daughters had not gone in much for that sort of thing, and Mrs Hook distrusted night air; it was also the first time that Chief Hook had ever been required to determine facts. He had been allowed to continue in office this long because his family was popular in town and the young men at the local bar liked him, and because his record for twenty years, of drunks locked up and petty thieves apprehended upon confession, had been immaculate. In a small town such as the one lying close to the Phillips Education Camp for Girls Twelve to Sixteen, crime is apt to take its form from the characters of the inhabitants, and a stolen dog or broken nose is about the maximum to be achieved ordinarily in the sensational line. No one doubted Chief Hook's complete inability to cope with the disappearance of a girl from the camp.

'You say she was going somewhere?' he asked Betsy, having put out his cigar in deference to the camp nurse, and visibly afraid that his questions would sound foolish to Old Jane; since Chief Hook was accustomed to speaking around his cigar, his voice without it was malformed, almost quavering.

'She said she had something to do,' Betsy told him.

'How did she say it? As though she meant it? Or do you think she was lying?'

'She just *said* it,' said Betsy, who had reached that point of stubbornness most thirteen-year-old girls have, when it seems that adult obscurity has passed beyond necessity. 'I *told* you eight times.'

Chief Hook blinked and cleared his throat. 'She sound happy?' he asked.

'Very happy,' said Betsy. 'She was singing all evening while I was trying to write in my Nature Book, is how I remember.'

'Singing?' said Chief Hook; it was not possible to him that a girl upon the very edge of disappearance had anything to sing about.

'Singing?' said Old Jane.

'Singing?' said Will Scarlett. 'You never told *us*.'

'Just sort of humming,' Betsy said.

'What tune?' said Chief Hook.

'Just *humming*,' Betsy said. 'I *told* you already, just *humming*. I nearly went crazy with my Nature Book.'

'Any idea where she was going?'

'No.'

An idea came to Chief Hook. 'What was she interested in?' he asked suddenly. 'You know, like sports, or boys, or anything.'

'There are no boys at the Phillips Educational Camp for Girls,' Old Jane said stiffly.

'She could have been *interested* in boys, though,' Chief Hook said. 'Or – like, well, books? Reading, you know? Or baseball, maybe?'

'We have not been able to find her Activity Chart,' the camp nurse said. 'Betsy, what recreational activity group was she in?'

'Golly.' Betsy thought deeply, and said, 'Dramatics? I think she went to Dramatics.'

'Which nature study group? Little John? Eeyore?'

'Little John,' said Betsy uncertainly. 'I *think*. I'm pretty sure she was in Dramatics because I think I remember her talking about *Six Who Pass While the Lentils Boil*.'

'That would be Dramatics,' Old Jane said. 'Surely.'

Chief Hook, who had begun to feel that this was all unnecessarily confusing, said, 'What about this singing?'

'There's singing in *Six Who Pass While the Lentils Boil*,' Will Scarlett said.

'How about boys?' said Chief Hook.

Betsy thought again, remembering as well as she could the sleeping figure in the other bed, the soiled laundry on the floor, the open suitcase, the tin boxes of cookies, the towels, the face cloths, the soap, the pencils . . . 'She had her own clock,' Betsy volunteered.

'How long have you roomed together?' Old Jane asked, and her voice was faintly sardonic, as though in deference to Chief Hook she were forced to restrain the saltier half of her remark.

'Last year and this year,' Betsy said. 'I mean, we both put in for rooms at the same time and so they put us together again. I mean, most of my friends are senior huntsmen and of course I can't room with them because they only put senior huntsmen with –'

'We know.' Old Jane was beginning to sound shrill. 'Any mail?'

'I don't know about that,' Betsy said. 'I was always reading my own mail.'

'What was she wearing?' Chief Hook asked.

'I don't know,' Betsy said. 'I didn't turn around when she left.' She looked from Chief Hook to Will Scarlett to Old Jane with a trace of impatience. 'I was doing my *Nature* Book.'

A search of the room, from which Betsy abstained and

which was carried on with enthusiasm by Old Jane and Will Scarlett and with some embarrassment by Chief Hook, showed that after Betsy's possessions had been subtracted from the medley, what was left was astonishingly little. There was a typed script of *Six Who Pass While the Lentils Boil*, and a poorly done painting of Echo Lake, which was part of the camp. There was a notebook, labeled, like Betsy's, 'Nature Book,' but it was unused, lacking the pressed wild-flowers and blue jay feathers; there was a copy of *Gulliver's Travels* from the camp library, which Old Jane felt might be significant. No one was able to tell certainly what she had been wearing, because the clothes in the closet were mostly Betsy's, and jackets or overshoes left in the room by Betsy's friends. In the drawers of the second dresser were a few scraps of underwear, a pair of heavy socks, and a red sweater which Betsy was fairly sure belonged to a woodsprite on the other side of camp.

A careful check-up of Recreational Activity lists showed that while she was listed for dramatics and nature study and swimming, her attendance at any of them was dubious; most of the counselors kept slipshod attendance records, and none of them could remember whether any such girl could have come on any given day.

'I'm almost sure I remember *her*, though,' Little John, an ardent girl of twenty-seven who wore horn-rimmed glasses and tossed her hair back from her face with a pretty gesture that somehow indicated that winters she wore it decently pinned up, told Chief Hook. 'I have an awfully good memory for faces, and I think I remember her as one of Rabbit's friends and relations. Yes, I'm sure I remember her, I have a good memory for faces.'

'Ah,' said the librarian, who was called Miss Mills when she was secretary to Old Jane, and the Snark when she was in the library, 'one girl is much like another, at *this* age. Their unformed minds, their unformed bodies, their little mistakes; we, too, were young once, Captain Hook.'

'Hell,' said the muscular young woman who was known as Tarzan because she taught swimming, 'did you ever look at fifty girls all in white bathing caps?'

'Elm?' said the nature study counselor, whose name was Bluebird. 'I mean, wasn't she an elm girl? Did a nice paper on blight? Or was it the other girl, Michaels? Anyway, whichever one it might have *been*, it was a nice job. Out of the ordinary for *us*, you know; remember it particularly. Hadn't noticed either of the girls to speak of – but if she's really gone, she might be up on Smoky Trail looking for fern; want the girls to make a special topic of fern and mushroom.' She stopped and blinked, presumably taking in a new supply of chlorophyll. 'Fern,' she said. 'Pays to know plenty about fern.'

'Few of them have any talent, anyway,' the painting counselor said. 'In any of the progressive schools *this* sort of thing –' She gestured tiredly at the canvases propped up against tree stumps or stacked upon a rock, and moved her shoulders nervously under her brand new blue and yellow checked shirt. 'Interested *psychologically*, of course,' she added quickly. 'If I remember this girl, she did sort of vague stuff, almost *unwilling.* Rejection, almost – if I can find a picture you'll see right away what I mean.' She poked unenthusiastically among the canvases stacked on the rock, pulled her hand back and said, 'Why did I ever –' wiping wet paint off on her blue jeans. 'Funny,' she said, 'I could have taken an oath she had a canvas around here somewhere. Sort of vague stuff, though – no sense of design, no eye.'

'Did she *ever*,' Chief Hook asked Betsy, 'ever ever *ever* mention anyplace she might want to go? Some foreign country, maybe?'

Old Jane's voice had an odd tone. 'The parents are arriving tomorrow.'

Chief Hook rubbed his forehead nervously. 'Lost a hunter last fall on Bad Mountain,' he suggested.

It was decided to search Bad Mountain, and then, unexpectedly, a house-to-house canvass along the road leading to Bad Mountain uncovered an honest clue. A housewife, glancing out her window to see if her husband was coming home from a poker game, had seen, she thought, the figure of a girl moving along the road, lighted occasionally by the headlights of passing cars.

'I couldn't *swear* it was a girl, though,' the housewife persisted nervously. 'That is, nights when Jim is out playing, I go to bed, and this night I was only up on account we had fried clams for supper, and I like clams but they don't –'

'What was she wearing?' Chief Hook demanded.

The woman thought. 'Well,' she said finally, 'the reason I figured she was one of those girls from the camp was she was wearing pants. But then, it could have been a man, you see, or a boy. Only somehow I sort of figured it was a girl.'

'Did she have on a coat? Hat?'

'A coat, I think,' the woman said, 'leastways, one of those short jackets. She was going up the road toward Jones Pass.'

Jones Pass led to Bad Mountain. It was not possible to get a picture of the girl; the picture on her camp application blank was so blurred that it resembled a hundred other girls in the camp; it was assumed, however, from the picture, that she had dark hair. A man was discovered who had given a ride to a girl hitchhiking on the road to Jones Pass; she had dark hair and was wearing blue jeans and a short tan leather jacket.

'I don't think she was a *camp* girl, though,' the man added earnestly, 'not the way she talked, she wasn't any girl from Phillips Camp, not *her*,' he said, and looked at Chief Hook, 'Bill, you remember that youngest girl over to Ben Hart's?'

Chief Hook sighed. 'You see anyone else driving down the road?' he asked. The man shook his head emphatically.

One of the junior counselors at the camp, who went by the name of Piglet, had been driving home late from town that night and at one point in the road near Jones Pass had had the clear impression of someone ducking behind a tree into the shadows. She was unable to say whether or not it had been a girl, or even whether it had been a person, but Chief Hook questioned her remorselessly.

'Can you face this girl's parents and honestly tell them you never lifted a finger to save her?' he demanded of Piglet. 'That innocent girl?'

Will Scarlett had shut herself into the infirmary and refused to let go of the phenobarbital; it was announced that she could not be disturbed. The press agent for the camp was taking all calls and managing the general search. Newspaper reporters were encouraged, but the seventeen-year-old son of the owner of the local paper was given first chance at all new developments; it occurred to this young man to ensure that a search be made over Bad Mountain by helicopter, and the camp went to tremendous expense to import one, although its six-day tour of the mountains showed nothing, and the son of the newspaper owner subsequently informed his father that he preferred having a plane to inheriting the paper, which went to a distant cousin. It was said that the girl had turned up in a town seventy-five miles away, dead drunk and trying to get a job in a shoe store, but the proprietor of the shoe store was unable to identify her picture, and it was later proven that the girl in question was actually the daughter of the mayor of that town. The widowed mother of the missing girl was prostrate with grief and under the care of a physician, but her uncle arrived at the camp and took personal charge of the search. The girls from the camp, led by the counselor in nature study and the senior huntsmen, had already gone over the mountain, looking for bent twigs and rock signs, but without success, although they had the assistance of chosen boy and girl scouts from the town. It was afterward told that Old Jane, indefatigable in leather puttees and a striped bandana and known to be extraordinarily susceptible to cold, had fallen down dead drunk in front of Chief Hook and had had to be carried home on a stretcher hastily improvised by the boy scouts, leading many people to believe that the girl's body had been found.

In the town it was generally believed that the girl had been killed and '*You* know,' and her body buried in a shallow grave somewhere east of Jones Pass, where the woods were deepest and ran downhill and for miles along the edge of Muddy River; knowing folk in town who had hunted the pass and Bad Mountain were quoted as saying that it would be mighty easy for anyone to miss a body in them woods; go ten feet off the path and you're lost, and the mud that deep already; it was generally conceded in the town that the girl had been followed in the darkness by a counselor from the camp, preferably one of the quiet ones, until she was out of sight or sound of help. The townspeople remembered their grandfathers had known of people disposed of in just that way, and no one had ever heard about it, either.

In the camp it was generally believed that one of the low bloods around the town – and try to match them for general vulgarity and insolence, and the generations of inbreeding that had led to idiocy in half the families and just plain filth in the rest – had enticed the girl off into an assignation on the mountain, and there outraged and murdered her and buried her body. The camp people believed that it was possible to dispose of a body by covering it with lime – heaven knew these country farmhands had enough lime in a barn to dispose of a dozen bodies – and that by the time the search started there wasn't enough left of the body to find. The camp people further believed that it was no more than you might expect of a retarded village in an isolated corner of the world, and they thought you might go far before you met up with a lower and a stupider group of clods; they pointed with triumph to the unusual lack of success of the Camp Talent Show early in the summer, to which the townspeople had been invited.

On the eleventh day of the search, Chief Hook, who perceived clearly that he might very well lose his job, sat down quietly for a conference with the girl's uncle, Old Jane, and Will Scarlett, who had emerged from the infirmary on the ninth day, to announce that she had for a long time been renowned as a minor necromancer and seer, and would gladly volunteer her services in any possible psychic way.

'I think,' said Chief Hook despondently, 'that we might as well give it up. The boy scouts quit a week ago, and today the girl scouts went.'

The girl's uncle nodded. He had gained weight on Mrs Hook's cooking and he had taken to keeping his belt as loose as Chief Hook's. 'We haven't made any progress, certainly,' he said.

'I told you to look under the fourth covered bridge from the blasted oak,' said Will Scarlett sullenly. 'I *told* you.'

'Miss Scarlett, *we* couldn't find no blasted oak,' Chief Hook said, 'and we looked and looked – No oaks in this part of the country at all,' he told the girl's uncle.

'Well, I told you to keep looking,' said the seer. 'I told you also look on the left-hand side of the road to Exeter.'

'We looked there, too,' Chief Hook said. 'Nothing.'

'You know,' said the girl's uncle, as though it were a

complete statement. He passed his hand tiredly across his forehead and looked long and soberly at Chief Hook, and then long and soberly at Old Jane, who sat quietly at her desk with papers in her hands. 'You know,' he said again. Then, addressing himself to Old Jane and speaking rapidly, he went on. 'My sister wrote to me today, and she's very upset. Naturally,' he added, and looked around at Old Jane, at Will Scarlett, at Chief Hook, all of whom nodded appreciatively, 'but listen,' he went on, 'what she says is that of course she loves Martha and all that, and of course *no* one would want to say anything about a girl like this that's missing, and probably had something horrible done to her . . .' He looked around again, and again everyone nodded. 'But she says,' he went on, 'that in spite of all that . . . well . . . she's pretty sure, what I mean, that she decided against Phillips Educational Camp for Girls. What I *mean*,' he said, looking around again, 'she has three girls and a boy, my sister, and of course we both feel *terribly* sorry and of course we'll still keep in our end of the reward and all that, but what I *mean* is . . .' He brushed his hand across his forehead again. '. . . What I mean is this. The oldest girl, that's Helen, she's married and out in San Francisco, so that's *her*. And – I'll show you my sister's letter – the second girl, that's Jane, well, *she's* married and *she* lives in Texas somewhere, has a little boy about two years old. And then the third girl – well, *that's* Mabel, and she's right at home with her mother, around the house and whatnot. Well – you see what I mean?'

No one nodded this time, and the girl's uncle went on nervously. 'The boy, *he's* in Denver, and his name is –'

'Never mind,' said Chief Hook. He rose wearily and reached into his pocket for a cigar. 'Nearly suppertime,' he said to no one in particular.

Old Jane nodded and shuffled the papers in her hand. 'I have all the records here,' she said. 'Although a girl named Martha Alexander applied for admission to the Phillips Educational Camp for Girls Twelve to Sixteen, her application was put into the file marked "possibly undesirable" and there is no record of her ever having come to the camp. Although her name has been entered upon various class lists, she is not noted as having participated personally in any activity; she has not, so far as we know, used any of her dining-room tickets or her privileges with regard to laundry and bus services, not to mention country dancing. She has not used the golf course nor the tennis courts, nor has she taken out any riding horses. She has never, to our knowledge, and our records are fairly complete, sir, attended any local church –'

'She hasn't taken advantage of the infirmary,' said Will Scarlett, 'or psychiatric services.'

'You see?' said the girl's uncle to Chief Hook.

'Nor,' finished Old Jane quietly, 'nor has she been vaccinated or tested for any vitamin deficiency whatsoever.'

A body that might have been Martha Alexander's was found, of course, something over a year later, in the late fall when the first light snow was drifting down. The body had been stuffed away among some thorn bushes, which none of the searchers had cared to tackle, until two small boys looking for a cowboy hideout had wormed their way through the thorns. It was impossible to say, of course, how the girl had been killed – at least Chief Hook, who still had his job, found it impossible to say – but it was ascertained that she had been wearing a black corduroy skirt, a reversible raincoat, and a blue scarf.

She was buried quietly in the local cemetery; Betsy, a senior huntsman the past summer but rooming alone, stood for a moment by the grave, but was unable to recognize any aspect of the clothes or the body. Old Jane attended the funeral, as befitted the head of the camp, and she and Betsy stood alone in the cemetery by the grave. Although she did not cry over her lost girl, Old Jane touched her eyes occasionally with a plain white handkerchief, since she had come up from New York particularly for the services.

## Journey with a Lady

'Honey,' Mrs Wilson said uneasily, 'are you *sure* you'll be all *right*?' 'Sure,' said Joseph. He backed away quickly as she bent to kiss him again. 'Listen, *Mother*,' he said. 'Everybody's *looking*.'

'I'm still not sure but what someone ought to go with him,' said his mother. 'Are you *sure* he'll be all right?' she said to her husband.

'Who, Joe?' said Mr Wilson. 'He'll be fine, won't you, son?'

'Sure,' said Joseph.

'A boy nine years old ought to be able to travel by himself,' said Mr Wilson in the patient tone of one who has been saying these same words over and over for several days to a nervous mother.

Mrs Wilson looked up at the train as one who estimates the probable strength of an enemy. 'But suppose something should *happen*?' she asked.

'Look, Helen,' her husband said, 'the train's going to leave in about four minutes. His bag is already on the train, Helen. It's on the seat where he's going to be sitting from now until he gets to Merrytown. I have spoken to the porter and I have given the porter a couple of dollars, and the porter has promised to keep an eye on him and see that he gets off the train with his bag when the train stops at Merrytown. He is nine years old, Helen, and he knows his name and where he's going and where he's supposed to get off, and Grandpop is going to meet him and will telephone you the minute they get to Grandpop's house, and the porter –'

'I know,' said Mrs Wilson, 'but are you sure he'll be all *right*?'

Mr Wilson and Joseph looked at one another briefly and then away.

Mrs Wilson took advantage of Joseph's momentary lapse of awareness to put her arm around his shoulders and kiss him again, although he managed to move almost in time and her kiss landed somewhere on the top of his head. '*Mother*,' Joseph said ominously.

'Don't want anything to happen to my little boy,' Mrs Wilson said with a brave smile.

'Mother, for heaven's *sake*,' said Joseph. 'I better get on the train,' he said to his father. 'Good idea,' said his father.

'Bye, Mother,' Joseph said, backing toward the train door; he took a swift look up and down the platform, and then reached up to his mother and gave her a rapid kiss on the cheek. 'Take care of yourself,' he said.

'Don't forget to telephone the minute you get there,' his mother said. 'Write me every day, and tell Grandma you're supposed to brush your teeth every night and if the weather turns cool –'

'Sure,' Joseph said. 'Sure, Mother.'

'So long, son,' said his father.

'So long, Dad,' Joseph said; solemnly they shook hands. 'Take care of yourself,' Joseph said.

'Have a good time,' his father said.

As Joseph climbed up the steps to the train he could hear his mother saying, 'And telephone us when you get there and be careful –'

'Goodbye, Goodbye,' he said, and went into the train. He had been located by his father in a double seat at the end of the car and, once settled, he turned as a matter of duty to the window. His father, with an unmanly look of concern, waved to him and nodded violently, as though to indicate that everything was going to be all right, that they had pulled it off beautifully, but his mother, twisting her fingers nervously, came close to the window of the train, and, fortunately unheard by the people within, but probably clearly audible to everyone for miles without, gave him at what appeared to be some length an account of how she had changed her mind and was probably going to come with him after all. Joseph nodded and smiled and waved and shrugged his shoulders to indicate that he could not hear, but his mother went on talking, now and then glancing nervously at the front of the train, as though afraid that the engine might start and take Joseph away before she had made herself absolutely sure that he was going to be all right. Joseph, who felt with some justice that in the past few days his mother had told him every conceivable pertinent fact about his traveling alone to his grandfather's, and her worries about same, was able to make out such statements as 'Be careful,' and 'Telephone us the minute you get there,' and 'Don't forget to write.' Then the train stirred, and hesitated, and moved slightly again, and Joseph backed away from the window, still waving and smiling. He was positive that what his mother was saying as the train pulled out was 'Are you *sure* you'll be all right?' She blew a kiss to him as the train started, and he ducked.

Surveying his prospects as the train took him slowly away from his mother and father, he was pleased. The journey should take only a little over three hours, and he knew the name of the station and had his ticket safely in his jacket pocket; although he had been reluctant to yield in any fashion to his mother's misgivings, he had checked several times, secretly, to make sure the ticket was safe. He had half a dozen comic books – a luxury he was not ordinarily allowed – and a choco-late bar; he had his suitcase and his cap, and he had seen personally to the packing of his first baseman's mitt. He had a dollar bill in the pocket of his pants, because his mother thought he should have some money in case – possibilities which had concretely occurred to her – of a train wreck (although his father had pointed out that in the case of a major disaster the victims were not expected to pay their own expenses, at least not before their families had been notified) or perhaps in the case of some vital expense to which his grandfather's income would not be adequate. His father had thought that Joe ought to have a little money by him in case he wanted to buy anything, and because a man ought not to travel unless he had money in his pocket. 'Might pick up a girl on the train and want to buy her lunch,' his father had said jovially and his mother, regarding her husband thoughtfully, had remarked, 'Let's hope *Joseph* doesn't do things like that,' and Joe and his father had winked at one another. So, regarding his comic books and his suitcase and his ticket and his chocolate bar, and feeling the imperceptible but emphatic presence of the dollar bill in his pocket, Joe leaned back against the soft seat, looked briefly out the window at the houses now moving steadily past, and said to himself, 'This is the life, boy.'

Before indulging in the several glories of comic books and chocolate, he spent a moment or so watching the houses of his hometown disappear beyond the train; ahead of him, at his grandfather's farm, lay a summer of cows and horses and probable wrestling matches in the grass; behind him lay school and its infinite irritations, and his mother and father. He wondered briefly if his mother was still looking after the train and telling him to write, and then largely he forgot her. With a sigh of pure pleasure he leaned back and selected a comic book, one that dealt with the completely realistic adventures of a powerful magician among hostile African tribes. This *is* the life, boy, he told himself again, and glanced again out the window to see a boy about his own age sitting on a fence watching the train go by. For a minute Joseph thought of waving down to the boy, but decided that it was beneath his dignity as a traveler; moreover, the boy on the fence was wearing a dirty sweatshirt, which made Joe move uneasily under his stiff collar and suit jacket, and he thought longingly of the comfortable old shirt with the insignia 'Brooklyn Dodger', which was in his suitcase. Then, just as the traitorous idea of changing on the train occurred to him, and of arriving at his grandfather's not in his good suit became a possibility, all sensible thought was driven from his mind by a cruel and unnecessary blow. Someone sat down next to him, breathing heavily, and from the quick flash of perfume and the movement of cloth that could only be a dress rustling Joe realized with a strong sense of injustice that his paradise had been invaded by some woman.

'Is this seat taken?' she asked.

Joe refused to recognize her existence by turning his head to look at her, but he told her sullenly, 'No, it's not.' Not taken, he was thinking, what did she think *I* was sitting here for? Aren't there enough old seats in the train she could go and sit in without taking mine?

He seemed to lose himself in contemplation of the scenery beyond the train window, but secretly he was wishing direly that the woman would suddenly discover she had forgotten her suitcase or find out she had no ticket or remember that she had left the bathtub running at home – anything, to get her off the train at the first station, and out of Joe's way.

'You going far?'

Talking, too, Joe thought, she has to take my seat and then she goes and talks my ear off, darn old pest. 'Yeah,' he said. 'Merrytown.'

'What's your name?'

Joe, from long experience, could have answered all her

questions in one sentence, he was so familiar with the series –
I'm nine years old, he could have told her, and I'm in the fifth
grade, and, no, I don't like school, and if you want to know
what I learn in school it's nothing because I don't like school
and I do like movies, and I'm going to my grandfather's house,
and more than anything else I hate women who come and sit
beside me and ask me silly questions and if my mother didn't
keep after me all the time about my manners I would probably
gather my things together and move to another seat and if
you don't stop asking me –

'What's your name, little boy?'

Little boy, Joe told himself bitterly, on top of everything
else, little boy.

'Joe,' he said.

'How old are you?'

He lifted his eyes wearily and regarded the conductor enter-
ing the car; it was surely too much to hope that this female
plague had forgotten her ticket, but could it be remotely possible that she was on the wrong train?

'Got your ticket, Joe?' the woman asked.

'Sure,' said Joe. 'Have you?'

She laughed and said – apparently addressing the conductor,
since her voice was not at this moment the voice women use
in addressing a little boy, but the voice that goes with speaking
to conductors and taxi drivers and salesclerks – 'I'm afraid I
haven't got a ticket. I had no time to get one.'

'Where are you going?' said the conductor.

Would they put her off the train? For the first time, Joe

turned and looked at her, eagerly and with hope. Would they possibly, hopefully, desperately, put her off the train? 'I'm going to Merrytown,' she said, and Joe's convictions about the generally weak-minded attitudes of the adult world were all confirmed. The conductor tore a slip from a pad he carried, punched a hole in it, and told the woman, 'Two seventy-three.' While she was searching her pocketbook for her money – if she knew she was going to have to buy a ticket, Joe thought disgustedly, whyn't she have her money ready? – the conductor took Joe's ticket and grinned at him. 'Your boy got *his* ticket all right,' he pointed out.

The woman smiled. 'He got to the station ahead of me,' she said.

The conductor gave her her change, and went on down the car. 'That was funny, when he thought you were my little boy,' the woman said.

'Yeah,' said Joe.

'What're you reading?'

Wearily, Joe put his comic book down.

'Comic,' he said.

'Interesting?'

'Yeah,' said Joe.

'Say, look at the policeman,' the woman said.

Joe looked where she was pointing and saw – he would not have believed this, since he knew perfectly well that most women cannot tell the difference between a policeman and a mailman – that it was undeniably a policeman, and that he was regarding the occupants of the car very much as though there might be a murderer or an international jewel thief riding calmly along on the train. Then, after surveying the car for a moment, he came a few steps forward to the last seat, where Joe and the woman were sitting.

'Name?' he said sternly to the woman.

'Mrs John Aldridge, Officer,' said the woman promptly. 'And this is my little boy, Joseph.'

'Hi, Joe,' said the policeman.

Joe, speechless, stared at the policeman and nodded dumbly.

'Where'd you get on?' the policeman asked the woman.

'Ashville,' she said.

'See anything of a woman about your height and build, wearing a fur jacket, getting on the train at Ashville?'

'I don't think so,' said the woman. 'Why?'

'Wanted,' said the policeman tersely.

'Keep your eyes open,' he told Joe. 'Might get a reward.'

He passed on down the car, and stopped occasionally to speak to women who seemed to be alone. Then the door at the far end of the car closed behind him and Joe turned and took a deep look at the woman sitting beside him. 'What'd you do?' he asked.

'Stole some money,' said the woman, and grinned.

Joe grinned back. If he had been sorely pressed, he might in all his experience until now have been able to identify only his mother as a woman both pretty and lovable; in this case, however – and perhaps it was enhanced by a sort of outlaw glory – he found the woman sitting next to him much more attractive than he had before supposed. She looked nice, she had soft hair, she had a pleasant smile and not a lot of lipstick and stuff on, and her fur jacket was rich and soft against Joe's hand. Moreover, Joe knew absolutely when she grinned at him that there were not going to be any more questions about nonsense like people's ages and whether they liked school, and he found himself grinning back at her in quite a friendly manner.

'They gonna catch you?' he asked.

'Sure,' said the woman. 'Pretty soon now. But it was worth it.'

'Why?' Joe asked; crime, he well knew, did not pay.

'See,' said the woman, 'I wanted to spend about two weeks having a good time there in Ashville. I wanted this coat, see? And I wanted just to buy a lot of clothes and things.'

'So?' said Joe.

'So I took the money from the old tightwad I worked for and I went off to Ashville and bought some clothes and went to a lot of movies and things and had a fine time.'

'Sort of a vacation,' Joe said.

'Sure,' the woman said. 'Knew all the time they'd catch me, of course. For one thing, I always knew I had to come home again. But it was worth it!'

'How much?' said Joe.

'Two thousand dollars,' said the woman.

'Boy!' said Joe.

They settled back comfortably. Joe, without more than a moment's pause to think, offered the woman his comic book about the African headhunters, and when the policeman came back through the car, eyeing them sharply, they were leaning back shoulder to shoulder, the woman apparently deep in African adventure, Joe engrossed in the adventures of a flying newspaper reporter who solved vicious gang murders.

'How is your book, Ma?' Joe said loudly as the policeman passed, and the woman laughed and said, 'Fine, fine.'

As the door closed behind the policeman the woman said softly, 'You know, I like to see how long I can keep out of their way.'

'Can't keep it up forever,' Joe pointed out.

'No,' said the woman, 'but I'd like to go back by myself and just give them what's left of the money. I had my good time.'

'Seems to me,' Joe said, 'that if it's the first time you did anything like this they probably wouldn't punish you so much.'

'I'm not ever going to do it again,' the woman said. 'I mean, you sort of build up all your life for one real good time like this, and then you can take your punishment and not mind it so much.'

'I don't know,' Joe said reluctantly, various small sins of his own with regard to matches and his father's cigars and other people's lunch boxes crossing his mind; 'seems to me that even if you do think *now* that you'll never do it again, sometimes – well, sometimes, you do it anyway.' He thought. 'I always *say* I'll never do it again, though.'

'Well, if you do it again,' the woman pointed out, 'you get punished twice as bad the next time.'

Joe grinned. 'I took a dime out of my mother's pocketbook once,' he said. 'But I'll never do *that* again.'

'Same thing I did,' said the woman.

Joe shook his head. 'If the policemen plan to spank you the way my father spanked me . . .' he said.

They were companionably silent for a while, and then the woman said, 'Say, Joe, you hungry? Let's go into the dining car.'

'I'm supposed to stay here,' Joe said.

'But I can't go without you,' the woman said. 'They think I'm all right because the woman they want wouldn't be traveling with her little boy.'

'Stop calling me your little boy,' Joe said.

'Why?'

'Call me your son or something,' Joe said. 'No more little-boy stuff.'

'Right,' said the woman. 'Anyway, I'm sure your mother wouldn't mind if you went into the dining car with *me*.'

'I bet,' Joe said, but he got up and followed the woman out of the car and down through the next car; people glanced up at them as they passed and then away again, and Joe thought triumphantly that they would sure stare harder if they knew that this innocent-looking woman and her son were outsmarting the cops every step they took.

They found a table in the dining car and sat down. The woman took up the menu and said, 'What'll you have, Joe?'

Blissfully, Joe regarded the woman, the waiters moving quickly back and forth, the shining silverware, the white table-cloth and napkins. 'Hard to say right off,' he said.

'Hamburger?' said the woman. 'Spaghetti? Or would you rather just have two or three desserts?'

Joe stared. 'You mean, like, just blueberry pie with ice cream and a hot fudge sundae?' he asked. 'Like that?'

'Sure,' said the woman. 'Might as well celebrate one last time.'

'When I took that dime out of my mother's pocketbook,' Joe told her, 'I spent a nickel on gum and a nickel on candy.'

'Tell me,' said the woman, leaning forward earnestly, 'the candy and gum – was it all right? I mean, the same as usual?'

Joe shook his head. 'I was so afraid someone would see me,' he said, 'I ate all the candy in two mouthfuls standing on the street and I was scared to open the gum at all.'

The woman nodded. 'That's why I'm going back so soon, I guess,' she said, and sighed.

'Well,' said Joe practically, 'might as well have blueberry pie first, anyway.'

They ate their lunch peacefully, discussing baseball and television and what Joe wanted to be when he grew up; once the policeman passed through the car and nodded to them cheerfully, and the waiter opened his eyes wide and laughed when Joe decided to polish off his lunch with a piece of watermelon. When they had finished and the woman had paid the check, they found that they were due in Merrytown in fifteen minutes, and they hurried back to their seat to gather together Joe's comic books and suitcase.

'Thank you very much for the nice lunch,' Joe said to the woman as they sat down again, and congratulated himself upon remembering to say it.

'Nothing at all,' the woman said. 'Aren't you my little boy?'

'Watch that little-boy stuff,' Joe said warningly, and she said, 'I mean, aren't you my son?'

The porter who had been delegated to keep an eye on Joe opened the car door and put his head in. He smiled reassuringly at Joe and said, 'Five minutes to your station, boy.'

'Thanks,' said Joe. He turned to the woman. 'Maybe,' he said urgently, 'if you tell them you're *really* sorry –'

'Wouldn't do at all,' said the woman. 'I really had a fine time.'

'I guess so,' Joe said. 'But you won't do it again.'

'Well, I knew when I started I'd be punished sooner or later,' the woman said.

'Yeah,' Joe said. 'Can't get out of it now.'

The train pulled slowly to a stop and Joe leaned toward the window to see if his grandfather was waiting.

'We better not get off together,' the woman said; 'might worry your grandpa to see you with a stranger.'

'Guess so,' said Joe. He stood up, and took hold of his suitcase. 'Goodbye, then,' he said reluctantly.

'Goodbye, Joe,' said the woman. 'Thanks.'

'Right,' said Joe, and as the train stopped he opened the door and went out onto the steps. The porter helped him to get down with his suitcase and Joe turned to see his grandfather coming down the platform.

'Hello, fellow,' said his grandfather. 'So you made it.'

'Sure,' said Joe. 'No trick at all.'

'Never thought you wouldn't,' said his grandfather. 'Your mother wants you to –'

'Telephone as soon as I get here,' Joe said. 'I know.'

'Come along, then,' his grandfather said. 'Grandma's waiting at home.'

He led Joe to the parking lot and helped him and his suitcase into the car. As his grandfather got into the front seat beside him, Joe turned and looked back at the train and saw the woman walking down the platform with the policeman holding her arm. Joe leaned out of the car and waved violently. 'So long,' he called.

'So long, Joe,' the woman called back, waving.

'It's a shame the cops had to get her after all,' Joe remarked to his grandfather.

His grandfather laughed. 'You read too many comic books, fellow,' he said. 'Everyone with a policeman isn't being arrested – he's probably her brother or something.'

'Yeah,' said Joe.

'Have a good trip?' his grandfather asked. 'Anything happen?'

Joe thought. 'Saw a boy sitting on a fence,' he said. 'I didn't wave to him, though.'

# Nightmare

It was one of those spring mornings in March; the sky between the buildings was bright and blue and the city air, warmed by motors and a million breaths, had a freshness and a sense of excitement that can come only from a breeze starting somewhere in the country, far away, and moving into the city while everyone is asleep, to freshen the air for morning. Miss Toni Morgan, going from the subway to her office, settled a soft, sweet smile on her face and let it stay there while her sharp tapping feet went swiftly along the pavement. She was wearing a royal blue hat with a waggish red feather in it, and her suit was blue and her topcoat a red and gray tweed, and her shoes were thin and pointed and ungraceful when she walked; they were dark blue, with the faintest line of red edging the sole. She carried a blue pocketbook with her initials in gold, and she wore dark blue gloves with red buttons. Her topcoat swirled around her as she turned in through the door of the tall office building, and when she entered her office sixty floors above, she took her topcoat off lovingly and hung it precisely in the closet, with her hat and gloves on the shelf above; she was precise about everything, so that it was exactly nine o'clock when she sat down at her desk, consulted her memorandum pad, tore the top leaf from the calendar, straightened her shoulders, and adjusted her smile. When her employer arrived at nine-thirty, he found her typing busily, so that she was able to look up and smile and say, 'Good morning, Mr Lang,' and smile again.

At nine-forty Miss Fishman, the young lady who worked at the desk corresponding to Miss Morgan's, on the other side of the room, phoned in to say that she was ill and would not be in to work that day. At twelve-thirty Miss Morgan went out to lunch alone, because Miss Fishman was not there. She had a bacon, tomato, and lettuce sandwich and a cup of tea in the drugstore downstairs, and came back early because there was a letter she wanted to finish. During her lunch hour she noticed nothing unusual, nothing that had not happened every day of the six years she had been working for Mr Lang.

At two-twenty by the office clock Mr Lang came back from lunch; he said, 'Any calls, Miss Morgan?' as he came through the door, and Miss Morgan smiled at him and said, 'No calls, Mr Lang.' Mr Lang went into his private office, and there were no calls until three-oh-five, when Mr Lang came out of his office carrying a large package wrapped in brown paper and tied with an ordinary strong cord.

'Miss Fishman here?' he asked.

'She's ill,' Miss Morgan said, smiling. 'She won't be in today.'

'Damn,' Mr Lang said. He looked around hopefully. Miss Fishman's desk was neatly empty; everything was in perfect order and Miss Morgan sat smiling at him. 'I've got to get this package delivered,' he said. 'Very important.' He looked at

Miss Morgan as though he had never seen her before. 'Would it be asking too much?' he asked.

Miss Morgan looked at him courteously for a minute before she understood. Then she said, 'Not at all,' with an extremely clear inflection, and stirred to rise from her desk.

'Good,' Mr Lang said heartily. 'The address is on the label. Way over on the other side of town. Downtown. You won't have any trouble. Take you about' – he consulted his watch – 'about an hour, I'd say, all told, there and back. Give the package directly to Mr Shax. No secretaries. If he's out, wait. If he's not there, go to his home. Call me if you're going to be more than an hour. Damn Miss Fishman,' he added, and went back into his office.

All up and down the hall, in offices directed and controlled by Mr Lang, there were people alert and eager to run errands for him. Miss Morgan and Miss Fishman were only the receptionists, the outer bulwark of Mr Lang's defence. Miss Morgan looked apprehensively at the closed door of Mr Lang's office as she went to the closet to get her coat. Mr Lang was being left defenceless, but it was spring outside, she had her red topcoat, and Miss Fishman had probably run off under cover of illness to the wide green fields and buttercups of the country. Miss Morgan settled her blue hat by the mirror on the inside of the closet door, slid luxuriously into her red topcoat, and picked up her pocketbook and gloves, and put her hand through the string of the package. It was unexpectedly light. Going toward the elevator, she found that she could carry it easily with the same hand that held her pocketbook, although its bulk would be awkward on the bus. She glanced at the address: 'Mr Ray Shax', and a street she had never heard of.

Once in the street in the spring afternoon, she decided to ask at the newspaper stand for the street; the little men in newspaper stands seem to know everything. This one was particularly nice to her, probably because it was spring. He took out a little red book that was a guide to New York, and searched through its columns until he found the street.

'You ought to take the bus on the corner,' he said. 'Going across town. Then get a bus going downtown until you get to the street. Then you'll have to walk, most likely. Probably a warehouse.'

'Probably,' Miss Morgan agreed absently. She was staring behind him, at a poster on the inside of the newspaper stand. 'Find Miss X,' the poster said in screaming red letters, 'Find Miss X. Find Miss X. Find Miss X.' The words were repeated over and over, each line smaller and in a different color; the bottom line was barely visible. 'What's that Miss X thing?' Miss Morgan asked the newspaperman. He turned and looked over his shoulder and shrugged. 'One of them contest things,' he said.

Miss Morgan started for the bus. Probably because the poster had caught her eye, she was quicker to hear the sound truck; a voice was blaring from it: 'Find Miss X! Win a mink coat valued at twelve thousand dollars, a trip to Tahiti; find Miss X.'

Tahiti, Miss Morgan thought, on a day like this. She went

swiftly down the sidewalk, and the sound truck progressed along the street, shouting, 'Miss X, find Miss X. She is walking in the city, she is walking alone; find Miss X. Step up to the girl who is Miss X, and say "You are Miss X," and win a complete repainting and decorating job on your house, win these fabulous prizes.'

There was no bus in sight and Miss Morgan waited on the corner for a minute before thinking, I have time to walk a ways in this lovely weather. Her topcoat swinging around her, she began to walk across town to catch a bus at the next corner.

The sound truck turned the corner in back of her; it was going very slowly, and she outdistanced it in a minute or so. She could hear, far away, the announcer's voice saying, '. . . and all your cosmetics for a year.'

Now that she was aware of it, she noticed that there were 'Find Miss X' posters on every lamppost; they were all like the one in the newsstand, with the words running smaller and smaller and in different colors. She was walking along a busy street, and she lingered past the shopwindows, looking at jewelry and custom-made shoes. She saw a hat something like her own, in a window of a store so expensive that only the hat lay in the window, soft against a fold of orange silk. Mine is almost the same, she thought as she turned away, and it cost only four ninety-eight. Because she lingered, the sound truck caught up with her; she heard it from a distance, forcing its way through the taxis and trucks in the street, its loudspeaker blaring music, something military. Then the announcer's voice began again: 'Find Miss X, find Miss X. Win fifty thousand dollars in cash;

Miss X is walking the streets of the city today, alone. She is wearing a blue hat with a red feather, a reddish tweed topcoat, and blue shoes. She is carrying a blue pocketbook and a large package. Listen carefully. Miss X is carrying a large package. Find Miss X, find Miss X. Walk right up to her and say "You are Miss X," and win a new home in any city in the world, with a town car and chauffeur, win all these magnificent prizes.'

Any city in the world, Miss Morgan thought, I'd pick New York. Buy me a home in New York, mister, I'd sell it for enough to buy all the rest of your prizes.

Carrying a package, she thought suddenly, *I'm* carrying a package. She tried to ease the package around so she could carry it in her arms, but it was too bulky. Then she took it by the string and swung it as close to her side as she could; must be a thousand people in New York right now carrying large packages, she thought; no one will bother me. She could see the corner ahead where her bus would stop, and she wondered if she wanted to walk another block.

'Say "You are Miss X,"' the sound truck screamed, 'and win one of these gorgeous prizes. Your private yacht, completely fitted. A pearl necklace fit for a queen. Miss X is walking the streets of the city, completely alone. She is wearing a blue hat with a red feather, blue gloves, and dark blue shoes.'

Good heavens, Miss Morgan thought; she stopped and looked down at her shoes; she was certainly wearing her blue ones. She turned and glared angrily at the sound truck. It was painted white, and had 'Find Miss X' written on the side in great red letters.

'Find Miss X,' the sound truck said.

Miss Morgan began to hurry. She reached the corner and mixed with the crowd of people waiting to get on the bus, but there were too many and the bus doors were shut in her face. She looked anxiously down the long block, but there were no other buses coming, and she began to walk hastily, going toward the next corner. I could take a taxi, she thought. That clown in the sound truck, he'll lose his job. With her free hand she reached up and felt that her hat was perched at the correct angle and her hair neat. I hope he *does* lose his job, she thought. What a thing to do! She could not help glancing over her shoulder to see what had become of the sound truck, and was shocked to find it creeping silently almost next to her, going along beside her in the street. When she looked around, the sound truck shouted, 'Find Miss X, find Miss X.'

'Listen,' Miss Morgan told herself. She stopped and looked around, but the people going by were moving busily without noticing her. Even a man who almost crashed into her when she stopped suddenly said only 'Excuse me,' and went on by without a backward look. The sound truck was stopped by traffic, up against the curb, and Miss Morgan went over to it and knocked on the window until the driver turned around.

'I want to speak to you,' Miss Morgan said ominously. The driver reached over and opened the door.

'You want something?' he asked wearily.

'I want to know why this truck is following me down the street,' Miss Morgan said; since she did not know the truck driver, and would certainly never see him again, she was possessed of great courage. She made her voice very sharp and said, 'What are you trying to do?'

'Me?' the truck driver said. 'Look, lady, I'm not following anybody. I got a route I gotta go. See?' He held up a dirty scrap of paper, and Miss Morgan could see that it was marked in pencil, a series of lines numbered like streets, although she was too far away to see what the numbers were. 'I go where it tells me,' the truck driver said insistently. 'See?'

'Well,' Miss Morgan said, her voice losing conviction, 'what do you mean, talking about people dressed like me? Blue hats, and so on?'

'Don't ask me,' the truck driver said. 'People hire this truck, I drive where they say. I don't have nothing to do with what happens back there.' He waved his hand toward the back of the truck, which was separated from him by a partition behind the driver's seat. The traffic ahead of him started and he said quickly, 'You want to know, you ask back there. Me, I don't hear it with the windows all shut.' He closed the door, and the truck moved slowly away. Miss Morgan stood on the curb, staring at it, and the loudspeaker began, 'Miss X is walking alone in the city.'

The nerve of him, Miss Morgan thought, reverting to a culture securely hidden beneath six years of working for Mr Lang, the goddamn nerve of him. She began to walk defiantly along the street, now slightly behind the sound truck. Serve them right, she thought, if anyone says to me, 'Are you Miss What's-her-name?' I'll say 'Why, yes, I am, here's your million dollars and you can go –'

'Reddish tweed topcoat,' the sound truck roared, 'blue shoes, blue hat.' The corner Miss Morgan was approaching was a hub corner, where traffic moved heavily and quickly, where crowds of people stood waiting to cross the street, where the traffic lights changed often. Suppose I wait on the corner, Miss Morgan thought, the truck will have to go on. She stopped on the corner near the sign 'bus stop,' and fixed her face in the blank expression of a bus rider, waiting for the sound truck to go on. As it turned the corner it shouted back at her, 'Find Miss X, find Miss X, she may be standing next to you now.'

Miss Morgan looked around nervously, and found she was standing next to a poster that began 'Find Miss X, find Miss X,' but went on to say, 'Miss X will be walking the streets of New York TODAY. She will be wearing blue – a blue hat, a blue suit, blue shoes, blue gloves. Her coat will be red and gray tweed. SHE WILL BE CARRYING A LARGE PACKAGE. Find Miss X, and claim the prizes.'

Good Lord, Miss Morgan thought, good Lord. A horrible idea crossed her mind: Could they sue her, take her into court, put her in jail for dressing like Miss X? What would Mr Lang say? She realized that she could never prove that she wore these clothes innocently, without criminal knowledge; as a matter of fact, she remembered that that morning, out in Woodside, while she was drinking her coffee, her mother had said, 'You won't be warm enough; the paper says it's going to turn cold later. Wear your heavy coat at least.' How would Miss Morgan ever be able to explain to the police that the spring weather had caught her, made her take her new coat instead of her old one? How could she prove anything? Cold fear caught Miss Morgan, and she began to walk quickly, away from the poster. Now she realized that there were posters everywhere: on the lampposts, on the sides of the buildings, blown up huge against the wall of a high building. I've got to do something right away, she thought, no time to get back home and change.

Trying to do so unobtrusively, she slid off her blue gloves and rolled them up and put them into her pocketbook. The pocketbook itself she put down behind the package. She buttoned her coat to hide the blue suit, and thought, I'll go into a ladies' room somewhere and take the feather out of my hat; if they know I tried to look different, they can't blame me. Ahead of her on the sidewalk she saw a young man with a microphone; he was wearing a blue suit and she thought humorously, put a blue hat on him and he'd do, when she realized that he was trying to stop people and talk about Miss X.

'Are you Miss X?' he was saying. 'Sorry, lady, red topcoat, you know, and carrying a package. Are you Miss X?' People were walking wider to avoid him, and he called to ladies passing, and sometimes they looked at him curiously. Now and then, apparently, he would catch hold of someone and try to ask them questions, but usually the women passed him without looking, and the men glanced at him once, and then away. He's going to catch me, Miss Morgan thought in panic, he's going to speak to *me*. She could see him looking through the crowds while he said into the microphone, loudly enough so that anyone passing could hear, 'Miss X is due to come down this street, folks, and it's about time for Miss X to be passing by here. She'll be along any minute, folks, and maybe you'll be the one who walks up to her and says "Are you Miss X?" and then you'll get those beautiful awards, folks, the golden tea service, and the library of ten thousand of the world's greatest books, folks, ten thousand books, and fifty thousand dollars. All you have to do is find Miss X, folks, just find the one girl who is walking around this city alone, and all you have to do is say "You are Miss X," folks, and the prizes are yours. And I'll tell you, folks, Miss X is now wearing her coat buttoned up so you can't see her blue suit, and she's taken off her gloves. It's getting colder, folks, let's find Miss X before her hands get cold without her gloves.'

He's going to speak to me, Miss Morgan thought, and she slipped over to the curb and signaled wildly for a taxi. 'Taxi,' she called, raising her voice shrilly, 'taxi!' Over her own voice she could hear the man with the microphone saying, 'Find Miss X, folks, find Miss X.' When no taxi would stop, Miss Morgan hurried to the other side of the sidewalk, next to the buildings, and tried to slip past the man at the microphone. He saw her, and his eyes jeered at her as she went by. 'Find Miss X, folks,' he said, 'find the poor girl before her hands get cold.'

I must be crazy, Miss Morgan thought. I'm just getting self-conscious because I'm tired of walking. I'll definitely get a taxi on the next corner.

'Find Miss X,' the sound truck shouted from the curb next to her.

'She's gone past here now,' the man with the microphone said behind her, 'she's passed us now, folks, but she's gone on down the street, find Miss X, folks.'

'Blue hat,' the sound truck said, 'blue shoes, carrying a large package.' Miss Morgan went frantically out into the street, not looking where she was going, crossed directly in front of the sound truck, and reached the other side, to meet a man wearing a huge cardboard poster saying 'Miss X, Miss X, find Miss X. CARRYING A LARGE PACKAGE. Blue shoes, blue hat, red and gray tweed coat, CARRYING A LARGE PACKAGE.' The man was distributing leaflets right and left, and people let them fall to the ground without taking them. Miss Morgan stepped on one of the leaflets and 'Find Miss X' glared up at her from the ground under her foot.

She was going past a millinery shop, when she had a sudden idea; moving quickly, she went inside, into the quiet. There were no posters in there, and Miss Morgan smiled gratefully at the quiet-looking woman who came forward to her. They don't do much business in *here*, Miss Morgan thought, they're so eager for customers, they come out right away. Her well-bred voice came back to her; 'I beg your pardon,' she said daintily, 'but would it be possible, do you think, for you to let me have either a hat bag or a hatbox?'

'A hatbox?' the woman said vaguely. 'You mean, empty?'

'I'd be willing to purchase it, of *course*,' Miss Morgan said, and laughed lightly. 'It just so happens,' she said, 'that I have decided to carry my hat in this beautiful weather, and one feels so foolish going down the street *carrying* a hat. So I thought a bag . . . or a hatbox . . .'

The woman's eyes lowered to the package Miss Morgan was carrying. 'Another package?' she asked.

Miss Morgan made a nervous gesture of putting the package behind her, and said, her voice a little sharper, 'Really, it doesn't seem like such a *strange* thing to *ask*. A hatbox or a bag.'

'Well . . .' the woman said. She turned to the back of the shop and went to a counter behind which were stacked piles of hatboxes. 'You see,' she said, 'I'm alone in the shop right now, and around here very often people come in just to make nuisances of themselves. There've been at least two burglaries in the neighborhood since we've been here, you know,' she added, looking uneasily at Miss Morgan.

'Really?' Miss Morgan said, her voice casual. 'And how long, may I ask, have you been here?'

'Well . . .' the woman said. 'Seventeen years.' She took down a hatbox, and then, suddenly struck with an idea, said, 'Would you like to look at some hats while you're here?'

Miss Morgan started to say no, and then her eye was caught by a red and gray caplike hat, and she said with mild interest, 'I might just try *that* one on, if I might.'

'Indeed, yes,' the woman said. She reached up and took the hat off the figure that held it. 'This is one of our best numbers,' she said, and Miss Morgan sat down in front of a mirror while the woman tried the hat on her.

'It's lovely on you,' the woman said, and Miss Morgan nodded. 'It's just the red in my coat,' she said, pleased.

'You really ought to wear a red hat with that coat,' the woman said.

Miss Morgan thought suddenly, what would Mr Lang say if he knew I was in here trying on hats when I'm supposed to be going on his errands. 'How much is it?' she asked hastily.

'Well . . .' the woman said. 'Eight ninety-five.'

'It's *far* too much for this hat,' Miss Morgan said. 'I'll just take the box.'

'That's eight ninety-five *with* the box,' the woman said unpleasantly.

Helplessly, Miss Morgan stared from the woman to the mirror to the package she had put down on the counter. There was a ten-dollar bill in her pocketbook. 'All right,' she said finally. 'Put my old hat in a box and I'll wear this one.'

'You'll never be sorry you bought that hat,' the woman said. She picked up Miss Morgan's blue hat and set it inside a box. While she was tying the box she said cheerfully, 'For a minute I was afraid you were one of the sort comes into a shop like this for no good. *You* know what I mean. Do you know, we've had two burglaries in the neighborhood since we've been here?'

Miss Morgan took the hatbox out of her hand and handed her the ten-dollar bill. 'I'm in rather a hurry,' Miss Morgan said. The woman disappeared behind a curtain at the back of the shop and came back after a minute with the change. Miss Morgan put the change in her pocketbook; I won't have enough for a taxi there and back, she thought.

Wearing the new hat, and carrying the hatbox and her pocketbook and the package, she left the shop, while the woman stared curiously after her. Miss Morgan found that she was a block and a half away from her bus stop, so she started again for it, and she was nearly on the corner before the sound truck came out of a side street, blaring, 'Find Miss X, find Miss X, win a Thoroughbred horse and a castle on the Rhine.'

Miss Morgan settled herself comfortably inside her coat. She had only to cross the street to get to her bus stop, and the bus was coming; she could see it a block away. She stopped to get the fare out of her pocketbook, shifting the package and the hatbox to do so, when the sound truck went slowly past her, shouting, 'Miss X has changed her clothes now, but she is still walking alone through the streets of the city, find Miss X! Miss X is now wearing a gray and red hat, and is carrying *two* packages; don't forget, *two* packages.'

Miss Morgan dropped her pocketbook and the hatbox, and stopped to pick up the small articles that had rolled out of her pocketbook, hiding her face. Her lipstick was in the gutter, her compact lay shattered, her cigarettes had fallen out of the case and rolled wide. She gathered them together as well as she could and turned and began to walk back the way she had come. When she came to a drugstore she went inside and to the phones. By the clock in the drugstore she had been gone just an hour and was only three or four blocks away from her office. Hastily, her hatbox and the package on the floor of the phone booth, she dialed her office number. A familiar voice answered – Miss Martin in the back room, Miss Walpole? – and Miss Morgan said, 'Mr Lang, please?'

'Who is calling, please?'

'This is Toni Morgan. I've got to speak to Mr Lang right away, please.'

'He's busy on another call. Will you wait, please?'

Miss Morgan waited; through the dirty glass of the phone booth she could see, dimly, the line of the soda fountain, the busy clerk, the office girls sitting on the high stools.

'Hello?' Miss Morgan said impatiently. 'Hello, hello?'

'Who did you wish to speak to, please?' the voice said – it might have been Miss Kittredge, in accounting.

'Mr Lang, please,' Miss Morgan said urgently. 'It's important.'

'Just a moment, please.' There was silence, and Miss Morgan waited. After a few minutes impatience seized her again and she hung up and found another nickel and dialed the number again. A different voice, a man's voice this time, one Miss Morgan did not know, answered.

'Mr Lang, please,' Miss Morgan said.

'Who's calling, please?'

'This is Miss Morgan, I must speak to Mr Lang at once.'

'Just a moment, please,' the man said.

Miss Morgan waited, and then said, 'Hello? Hello? What *is* the matter here?'

'Hello?' the man said.

'Is Mr Lang there?' Miss Morgan said. 'Let me speak to him at once.'

'He's busy on another call. Will you wait?'

He's answering my other call, Miss Morgan thought wildly, and hung up. Carrying the package and the hatbox, she went out again into the street. The sound truck was gone and everything was quiet except for the 'Find Miss X' posters on all the lampposts. They all described Miss X as wearing a red and gray cap and carrying two packages. One of the prizes, she noticed, was a bulletproof car, another was a life membership in the stock exchange.

She decided that whatever else, she must get as far from the neighborhood as she could, and when a taxi stopped providentially to let off passengers at the curb next to her, she stepped in, and gave the driver the address on the package. Then she leaned back, her hatbox and the package on the seat next to her, and lit one of the cigarettes she had rescued when her pocketbook fell. I've been dreaming, she told herself, this has all been so silly. The thing she most regretted was losing her presence enough, first, to speak so to the driver of the sound truck, and then to drop her pocketbook and make herself conspicuous stooping to pick everything up on the street corner. As the taxi drove downtown she noticed the posters on every lamppost, and smiled. Poor Miss X, she thought, I wonder if they *will* find her?

'I'll have to stop here, lady,' the taxi driver said, turning around.

'Where are we?' Miss Morgan said.

'Times Square,' the driver said. 'No cars getting through downtown on account of the parade.'

He opened the door and held out his hand for her money. Unable to think of anything else to do, Miss Morgan paid him and gathered her hatbox and package together and stepped out of the taxi. The street ahead was roped off and policemen were guarding the ropes. Miss Morgan tried to get through the crowd of people, but there were too many of them and she was forced to stand still. While she was wondering what to do, she heard the sound of a band and realized that the parade was approaching. Just then the policeman guarding the curb opened the ropes to let traffic cross the street for the last time before the parade, and all the people who had been standing with Miss Morgan crossed to the other side and all the people who had been on the other side crossed to stand on Miss Morgan's side, turning in order to cross again on the side street at right angles to the way they had crossed before, but the policemen and the crowds held them back and they waited, impatient for the next crossing. Miss Morgan had been forced to the curb and now she could see the parade coming downtown. The band was leading the parade; twelve drum majorettes in scarlet jackets and skirts and wearing silver boots and carrying silver batons marched six abreast down the street, stepping high and flinging their batons into the air in unison; following them was the band, all dressed in scarlet, and on each of the big drums was written a huge X in scarlet. Following the band were twelve heralds dressed in black velvet, blowing on silver trumpets, and they were followed by a man dressed in black velvet on a white horse with red plumes on its head; the man was shouting, 'Find Miss X, find Miss X, find Miss X.'

Then followed a float preceded by two girls in scarlet who carried a banner inscribed in red, 'Win magnificent prizes', and the float represented, in miniature, a full symphony orchestra; all the performers were children in tiny dress suits, and the leader, who was very tiny, stood on a small platform on the float and led the orchestra in a small rendition of 'Afternoon of a Faun'; following this float was one bearing a new refrigerator, fifty times larger than life, with the door swinging open to show its shelves stocked with food. Then a float bearing a model of an airplane, with twelve lovely girls dressed as clouds. Then a float holding a golden barrel full of enormous dollar bills, with a grinning mannequin who dipped into the barrel, brought up a handful of the great dollar bills, and ate them, then dipped into the barrel again.

Following this float were all the Manhattan troops of Boy Scouts; they marched in perfect line, their leaders going along beside and calling occasionally, 'Keep it up, men, keep that step even.'

At this point the side street was allowed open for cross traffic, and all the people standing near Miss Morgan crossed immediately, while all the people on the other side crossed also. Miss Morgan went along with the people she had been standing with, and once on the other side, all these people continued walking downtown until they reached the next corner and were stopped. The parade had halted here, and Miss Morgan found that she had caught up with the float representing the giant refrigerator. Farther back, the Boy Scouts had fallen out of their even lines, and were pushing and laughing.

One of the children on the orchestra float was crying. While the parade halted, Miss Morgan and all the people she stood with were allowed to cross through the parade to the other side of the avenue. Once there, they waited to cross the next side street.

The parade started again. The Boy Scouts came even with Miss Morgan, their lines straightening, and then the cause of the delay became known; twelve elephants, draped in blue, moved ponderously down the street; on the head of each was a girl wearing blue, with a great plume of blue feathers on her head; the girls swayed and rocked with the motion of the elephants. Another band followed, this one dressed in blue and gold, but the big drums still said X in blue. A new banner followed, reading 'Find Miss X,' with twelve more heralds dressed in white, blowing on gold trumpets, and a man on a black horse who shouted through a megaphone, 'Miss X is walking the streets of the city, she is watching the parade. Look around you, folks.'

Then came a line of twelve girls, arm in arm, each one dressed as Miss X, with a red and gray hat, a red and gray tweed topcoat, and blue shoes. They were followed by twelve men each carrying two packages, the large brown package Miss Morgan was carrying, and the hatbox. They were all singing, a song of which Miss Morgan caught only the words 'Find Miss X, get all those checks.'

Leaning far out over the curb, Miss Morgan could see that the parade continued for blocks; she could see green and orange and purple, and far far away, yellow. Miss Morgan pulled uneasily at the sleeve of the woman next to her. 'What's the parade for?' she asked, and the woman looked at her.

'Can't hear you,' the woman said. She was a little woman, and had a pleasant face, and Miss Morgan smiled, and raised her voice to say, 'I said, how long is this parade going to last?'

'What parade?' she asked. '*That* one?' She nodded at the street. 'I haven't any idea, miss. I'm trying to get to Macy's.'

'Do you know anything about this Miss X?' Miss Morgan said daringly.

The woman laughed. 'It was over the radio,' she said. 'Someone's going to get a lot of prizes. You have to do some kind of a puzzle or something.'

'What's it for?' Miss Morgan asked.

'Advertising,' the woman said, surprised.

'Are *you* looking for Miss X?' Miss Morgan asked daringly.

The woman laughed again. 'I'm no good at that sort of thing,' she said. 'Someone in the company of the people putting it on always wins those things, anyway.'

Just then they were allowed to cross again, and Miss Morgan and the woman hurried across, and on down the next block. Walking beside the woman, Miss Morgan said finally, 'I think I'm the Miss X they're talking about, but I don't know why.'

The woman looked at her and said, 'Don't ask *me*,' and then disappeared into the crowd of people ahead.

Out in the street a prominent cowboy movie star was going by on horseback, waving his hat.

Miss Morgan retreated along a quiet side street until she

was far away from the crowds and the parade; she was lost, too far away from her office to get back without finding another taxi, and miles away from the address on the package. She saw a shoe repair shop, and struck by a sudden idea, went inside and sat down in one of the booths. The repairman came up to her and she handed him her shoes.

'Shine?' he said, looking at the shoes.

'Yes,' Miss Morgan said. 'Shine.' She leaned back in the booth, her eyes shut. She was vaguely aware that the repairman had gone into the back of the shop, that she was alone, when she heard a footstep and looked up to see a man in a blue suit coming toward her.

'Are you Miss X?' the man in the blue suit asked her.

Miss Morgan opened her mouth, and then said, 'Yes,' tiredly.

'I've been looking all over for you,' the man said. 'How'd you get away from the sound truck?'

'I don't know,' Miss Morgan said. 'I ran.'

'Listen,' the man said, 'this town's no good. No one spotted you.' He opened the door of the booth and waited for Miss Morgan to come.

'My shoes,' Miss Morgan said, and the man waved his hand impatiently. 'You don't need shoes,' he said. 'The car's right outside.'

He looked at Miss Morgan with yellow cat eyes and said, 'Come on, hurry up.'

She stood up and he took her arm and said, 'We'll have to do it again tomorrow in Chicago, this town stinks.'

*

That night, falling asleep in the big hotel, Miss Morgan thought briefly of Mr Lang and the undelivered package she had left, along with her hatbox, in the shoe repair shop. Smiling, she pulled the satin quilt up to her chin and fell asleep.